Annette Daniels Taylor

An imprint of Enslow Publishing

WEST **44** BOOKS™

Please visit our website, www.west44books.com.
For a free color catalog of all our high-quality books,
call toll free 1-800-542-2595 or fax 1-877-542-2596.

Cataloging-in-Publication Data

Names: Daniels Taylor, Annette
Title: Dreams on fire / Annette Daniels Taylor.
Description: New York : West 44, 2019. | Series: West 44 YA verse
Identifiers: ISBN 9781538382479 (pbk.) | ISBN 9781538382486
  (library bound) | ISBN 9781538383247 (ebook)
Subjects: LCSH: Children's poetry, American. | Children's poetry,
  English. | English poetry.
Classification: LCC PS586.3 D743 2019 | DDC 811'.60809282--dc23

First Edition

Published in 2019 by
Enslow Publishing LLC
101 West 23rd Street, Suite #240
New York, NY 10011

Copyright © 2019 Enslow Publishing LLC

Editor: Caitie McAneney
Designer: Seth Hughes

Printed in the United States of America

CPSIA compliance information: Batch #CS18W44: For further information contact
Enslow Publishing LLC, New York, New York at 1-800-542-2595.

*To the children and teens residing inside the
Erie County Youth Detention Center.
Write, dance, sing, and create out of there...*

For Bessie and Shanequa Daniels

Five-Year Nightmare

I am Shanequa Oni Stephens.
Michael is my father.
My father is my dad.
I love my daddy Michael,
no matter what Grandma says.

Daddy loves his little girls.
That's what our daddy says.
But our daddy made
a big mistake.
One of the biggest, I think,
dads can make.

The Deed

went down five years ago.
LaKecia was seven. I was ten.
Daddy shot and killed a man.
Here's the story I was told.
Daddy dreamed of being
a great piano-playing man.
Writing songs our mama, Lisa, would sing
when she headed the True Love band.

Home Filled with Sounds of Music

Every day,
every night.
Daddy wrote love songs.
Mama would sing them
just right.
Every rehearsal she'd sing
romantic melodies
of how perfect love could be.

One night
inside Pandora's Box,
a drunk put his hand on Mama.

Daddy kicked him out.
The band laughed.
Some drinks were drunk.
Rehearsal began again.

The door opened.
That man came back,
looking through
bloodshot eyes.

Threatening Daddy
with his gun.
Threatening Daddy
to end his life.

Folks dove.
To the floor they fled.
A practiced safety routine.

That man didn't know…

Daddy Carried a Gun

That's why that man is dead.

Lawyer:	*Self-defense!*
District Attorney:	*Concealed weapon. Murder, second degree!*
Daddy:	*Pick up your heads!*
Grandma:	*Pray up to the begotten Son.*
Mama:	*Hurting, need to forget…*

Daddy in prison.
Judge gave 25 years.
Good behavior lessens time,
not Mama's tears.

Daddy's Time

made Mama sick.
The sickest moms could be.
Mama wakes mid-morning,
tired
    sad
        depressed,
        face unwashed,
        hair matted & messed.

Doctor's medicine
has no more refills.
In the bedroom,
Mama smokes her own medicine.

Mama can't make breakfast.
Mama can't get dressed.
Mama turns on TV.
Mama goes to bed.

We Are Kitchen
Food Hunters

Empty refrigerator lights
show pantry cupboards
filled with dust and air.

Mama dresses up.
Lipstick, high-heeled boots,
braving the big-bad world.

I'll be right back!

That's what Mama says.
Mama walks out the front door.
She winks, blows us a kiss.

Don't Remember

whether we caught the kiss or not.
We both fell asleep waiting.

Garbage truck wake-up alarm
tells us
we're still home alone.

Next morning,
Grandma's key unlocks our door.

School called. Dropped a dime to Social Services!

Court took Mama's
parent rights away.

Grandma is named guardian
until our parents
satisfy the state.

Bidwell Academy for Girls Admission

Prompt:
What's Your Dream?

I dream
watching stars burn.
I dream blazing truth.
My dreams are
singed, charred,
scorched, and seared.
Fifty-cent plastic lighters
littering streets
fade hope's pathway.
But I
dream eyes open,
fingers on keyboards,
finding chords, dreaming melodies.
Finding words.
I dream goals,
gleaming glittering glowing.
Lighting moments.
I dream spirit building,
souls lifting,
hopes thunder.
With pens, with pencils,
I'm writing my dreams on fire.

Bedtime Stories

LaKecia and I each repeat grades
on account of school we missed.
Grandma says we should
read to *her*.

Whatever, don't matter,
as long as *we're* reading.

We say,
>   *Grandma, read to us.*

She'll
>   *hmph,*
make a fuss.
>   *Y'all children, I'm adult!*

Folks say,
>   *You and LaKecia so smart!*

Yeah, we read a lot!

LaKecia Looks

just like Mama.
Pretty, thin, high cheeks,
thick lips,
light butterscotch brown,
like they island born.
I'm just like Daddy.
Plain, thick, big eyes,
broad shoulders,
cocoa-colored brown.
Mainland born.
Def looking sisterly
when side by side
together, but
stupid folks say stuff like,
What happened to Shanequa?
LaKecia pretty. You must be smart!

Thinking I'm ugly
ain't permission to be mean.

Saturdays Are For

house cleaning,
ceiling to floor.
Gotta get grime from
crusty corner crevices.

Last little lady.
Lazy late LaKecia.
I'm up after Kirk Franklin
shout-sings sermons
through the speakers.

Saturday is pre-Sunday:
clean home, body, & mind.
Surrounding space with singing sounds.
Harmony greets Grandma with smiles!

I Am Waffle Maker

since our daddy's
state
sentenced
separation.

His waffles were better.
Haven't gotten his
"just right-ness" yet.
More practice figures it out,
Grandma says.

Saturday mornings,
using Dad's old waffle iron.
Breakfast test success—
or error.

Afterwards, we
bleach, dust, soak, wash,
lavender Pine-Sol
the entire apartment.

Hair-Do Time!

Grandma says,
> *"Ratchet-ness" a sin.*

She says,
> *Not letting y'all look*
> *tore up in church tomorrow!*

She fixes our heads up just right.
This week, designer butterfly
cornrows flutter atop
our decorated heads!

Grandma should've went to
beauty school.
Got certified, licensed, legal.
She studies up,
perfecting
new hairstyle skills.
Watching YouTube lessons
on her phone.

Thursday nights, some Fridays,
every Saturday afternoon,
"Cora's Kitchen Salon" full up with
neighborhood-discount
wannabe-looking-like
reality show divas!

Church ladies, girls I know,
women who say,

Used to know your mama...

And others who say,
> *Baby, how your daddy doing?*
> *We are praying for him...*

Just making small talk.
Some folks don't know how
to say nothing

when they get a
curl & press,
extensions, braids, or weaves.

Driving Dreams

Grandma's saving
for a car.
Got half already.

      Making an investment,
she says.
Soon, she gonna drive to work.
Drive to the supermarket.
Drive to the doctor office.
Drive to church.
Drive to the laundromat.
Drive to school.
Drive to the art museum.
Drive to the zoo.
Drive to pick apples
at a farm.
Drive to the river to see the boats!

Maybe drive to visit Daddy
if she lets us.

Grandma say,
      I don't visit inside jails.
      Never have, never will.
      Your daddy knew that
      ever since he was little!

We ain't seen Daddy in four years.

Pastor's Blessing

Pastor Gorham tells congregation,

> *Pray for our own Shanequa Stephens.*
> *Lord blessing her gifts with opportunity!*

He takes up offering for me.
Gotta gift card
for new clothes.
    School supplies,
    filled bookbag.
Says,
> *Church, we don't want her*
> *feeling less than a child of God*
> *when she over there,*
> *do we?*

I'm Stranger

Grandma says,

> *Pastor's praying, and your grades,*
> *get you into Bidwell Academy for Girls.*
> *Do your job and don't spoil it.*

I say,
> *Yes, Grandma.*

She says,
> *Mind yourself.*
> *Folks still folks.*
> *They like being with they own.*
> *Strangers be strange to them.*

Knowing I'm the stranger
I always feel strange.

First Day

New gift card clothes!
Promise to self:
hide business,
hold dreams.

Knees covered,
code of dress.
Be on fleek and
look your best.

Their phones smartest,
newest, freshest.
Hide that stupid
candy-bar phone mess.

Don't look charity-like,
extra.
First school day
everybody sees
the darkest girl.

Watch and study.
Keep fresh and clean.

Dreaming in My City

Took the bus,
then train.
To get to Bidwell Academy for Girls.
Tree-lined streets,
air smells sweet.
Women walk cute doggies,
wearing North Face and Nikes.
Cute pizza parlors.
Cute dress stores.
Cute coffee shops.
Cute-looking street.
Cute bookstores,
reflecting me.
Already out of place
in my city.

Fairytale School

The most beautiful place ever.
Like movies.
Like fairytales.
Like make-believe dreams.
Bidwell Academy for Girls,
the most beautiful place ever.
I'm dreaming
of carved oak doors.
Shiny marble floors.
Real art
by real artists,
not students.
Grand fireplace in the library.
Fancy glass ceiling lamps
dance reflections across my face.

Shanequa Defined

Mrs. Miller: Shay-nee-Kwa Oh-Neye Stee-fans?

Shanequa: *Sha-Nee-Kwa Oh-Nee Stee-fans.*

Mrs. Miller: That's an interesting name.

Ashley: Yeah, interesting. *(snicker, snicker)*

Mrs. Miller: Ashley, would you like to address the entire class?

Ashley: I was just saying how pretty Shanequa's name is. Does it mean something?

Shanequa: Yeah...

Shanequa Means

God is gracious.

Oni means
big sister in Korean
and *god of disaster* in Japanese.

Ashley: Are you a big sister or a disaster?

I guess, in truth,
I am both.

Trauma Dreams

Sometimes at night,
dreams are like, empty.
When all's quiet,
dreaming is like, being.
Sometimes at night,
dreams are like,
creepers hiding in mirrors.

Dreams are like, dark places.
Re-memor-ing terrors.

Sometimes at night,
big burnt-eyed
zombies chase me
in mirrors of fire,
in reflections,
like being in dreams.

LaKecia's Trauma Dreams

LaKecia dreams of dark voices.
Heavy with trouble.
Dark surprises.
Ears open before eyes.
Sounds heard before sights seen.
LaKecia sounds alarms.
I am holding LaKecia.
Closely shielding fears while swimming
through trauma tears.
Ears ring brightly,
my eyes stuck shut,
forced open by
LaKecia dreaming of
sorrow knocking on
our front door, blanketing Mama's cries.
Dreams are monsters.
Daddy on the floor.
Four policemen. Knees in his back.
Curious ogres, before ears
alert sound, before sight
awakens memory.

Oni Bedside Manner

I'm on lifeguard sister duty.
Got my orders—
LaKecia's bedside.

Her small voice shaking, we rock
                    back to sleep.
                    The same dream.
                    The same
                    night-terror,
                    rerun,
                            guns pointing.

Silver handcuffs on Daddy's wrists.
Nightmare reruns.
LaKecia crying, re-running to Daddy.
Policemen push her.
LaKecia falls.
I'm frozen.
Mama in between, cradles LaKecia,
cussing police.

Daddy Doesn't Argue

Daddy doesn't fight.
Police beat him anyway.
Mama in handcuffs.
Police say my mama is *dangerous. Gonna hurt somebody!*
Threaten to arrest her.
They say: *For your own good!*

Police threaten to take us.
Threaten **C**hild **P**rotective **S**ervices.
Mama yells, *Call Grandma!*
Grabbing LaKecia,
I run to Mama and Daddy's room.

I lock the door, call Grandma.
Tell her get here, police arresting Daddy,
Mama in handcuffs.

Tell her we real, real scared.

Miss Mary

brought Aaliyah over,
wants some crochet extensions.
Aaliyah says,
>   *That's Shanequa's thing,*
not looking at Grandma.
>   *Your braids don't pull tight.*
Her basketball's an extension of her arm.
Steady ball dribbling,
hollow rhythmic beat.

Mad Respect

Grandma says,
> *Aaliyah, stop bouncing. Ain't the playground!*
Aaliyah polite, all,
> *Yes, ma'am.*

You can front in the streets,
but Grandma Cora demands mad respect from young folks.
Polite attitude gets you hair credit when money's funny.
Best know how to speak.

Aaliyah Got Mad Tall

She's point guard on East basketball team.
Miss Mary says,
>   *If she fails English and math,*
>   *I'm taking that ball*
>   *and the team's in the past!*
We were besties in elementary school,
but in middle,
she found a different crew after
her dad got snatched by a bullet.

She stopped talking some, too.

Miss Mary ask,
>   *Shanequa, you going to that bougie school? Help Aaliyah.*
>   *I'll pay you to!*

Grandma Gives the Look

I ain't got no choice.

Yes, Miss Mary.
I say,
What day's good, Aaliyah?

> *I can do whenever after 4:00.*

Wanna meet at the Center when I pick up LaKecia?

> *Yeah, a'ight?*

Monday and Wednesday? Let's meet at 4:30.

> *A'ight, that's bet.*

Aaliyah's Late

Finish homework, I wait.
Eat chicken fingers and fries with LaKecia.
Hear a gym basketball game.
Call out Aaliyah's name.
She stops.

Oh snap! My bad, Shanequa. I forgot.

Word. Look like you was ducking me?

Look, just call this a wrap, you feel me?

Can't lie to Miss Mary.

Say nothin', then.

The team'll cut you.

No nevermind, already a baller.

Pulling out cash, Aaliyah hands me a twenty.

That cover your tutor fee?

Miss Precious Writes Poetry

Miss Precious a poet.
Miss Precious the only black teacher.
Miss Precious asks for focus.

> She's a visiting artist.
> Writing poems every day.
> Her job's to inspire young writers,
> to create stories on the page.

Her skin is dark like coffee,
with a splash of cream swirlin'.
Eyes big and round like Grandad's,
before cancer got him.

> She reads us a poem,
> about claiming who you are.
> Challenge your outer vision,
> propel your inner star.

Gives us an assignment,
a poem telling who we are.
I'm afraid to be truthful.
Won't reveal private scars.

I Am by Shanequa O. Stephens

I am the oldest daughter, an Oni.
> I wonder how to walk through fire.
> I hear wind whispering under streetlamps.
> I see secrets shaking temptation's hands.

I want today to divorce history.
> I am the oldest daughter, an Oni.
> I play pretend with LaKecia.

I touch photos of our mother.
> I cry remembering she's gone.
> I worry if LaKecia sleeps enough.
> I am the oldest daughter, an Oni.

I feel handcuffs of responsibility.
> I understand roles change.
> I need to breathe childhood dreams.
> I say Mama still exists.

I am the oldest daughter, an Oni.

Funny How Folks Believe

in death.
Writing lies in poems
don't feel like *real* lying.
I never said Mama's dead.
They thought it because the words
I read.
Never said my mama died,
just said she wasn't here.
It's better folks believe she passed away

        instead of knowing she's a junk-head.

Miss Precious Talks After Class

Says,
> *I appreciate your poem.*

Says,
> *I'm sorry about your mother.*

Asks about my dad.
I shrug my shoulders,
look down at the floor.
Taste lies growing in my mouth.

He gone...

I get the faraway look.
Get teary-eyed
on account of
me lying.

Round My Way

Miss Precious, hand on my shoulder,
says,
>   *It's okay. I understand.*

But she don't.
Because
I'm lying.

She grew up round my way.
Buffalo, East Side, Grider & Delavan streets,
lived in foster homes.
Quoting Drake,
>   *Started from the bottom, now we're here.*

She's cool.
I'm a liar.

A Visiting Artist

is not a regular classroom teacher.
Miss Precious asks do I have computer, internet.
Bidwell Academy gives everyone a laptop.
I don't say I do my homework
at the community center where
LaKecia has after-school care.
We can't afford wi-fi.

Miss Precious says I'm gifted.
Says, *Keep on writing.*
Email new poems.
We can talk.
Her parents are not dead.
Orphan is sometimes defined by
feelings.
Her dad disappeared.
She's a jail-born baby.
County took her away from her mom.

Says, *Nobody wanted a*
            sickly crack-baby.
Hoping I'll reach out,
she says,
            I'm here for you.

If I need.
If I want.

Ashley

sits with me at lunch.
Says her mother died too.
Driving in a snowstorm.
Black ice, whiteout.

> *I get your poem.*
> *I get feeling alone.*
> *You are so lucky*
> *you have a sister,*
> *and you're not all alone.*

She's a residential student.
That means she lives at Bidwell Academy.
Boarding school.

Says,
> *My dad travels*
> *a lot for work.*
> *Been months since I've seen him,*
> *even during summer break.*
> *Wanna hang out later?*

Showed Grandma

the poem I wrote
for Miss Precious.

She says,
> That's nice, baby.
> Hang it on the refrigerator.

That's all she ever says.

Dad would OOH and AAH over
everything we did.
He would take out the camera
on his phone,
record an after-school performance.
He would post and share.

Grandma Brags

to all her Saturday clients
about her smart, talented grands.

But then she tells me cutting carrots
more important
than making poetic art!

> *Shanequa, start the rice.*
> *Read your story at dinner.*

Grandma only reads her phone,
the Bible, and bills.

LaKecia Liked

hearing her name in the poem.
Grandma didn't like
how it sounded like Mama's dead.

Even though I don't like one
bit how she let the devil rule her
world over being a good mother,
I don't approve of
writing stories like
she dead.
It's as good as lying.

Never Said She Was Dead, Grandma!

No, but it sounds like that what you saying.
What your teacher say about that?

She liked it. Said I have a gift.

Hmm. I think so too,
but you also got a
responsibility to do.
Say what's true, right?
It's your duty
to do well no matter what.
I'm counting on you.
Ignore distractions
for LaKecia and yourself.
Graduate!
A high school diploma—
you be the first!

Mama got a diploma.

She throws away gifts.
Be first in my family.
Believe you're worthy, girl.
You ain't have to lie to be liked!

Night at the Philharmonic

Going to the Philharmonic.
The best symphony in the city!
Grandma gave me permission.
It was a school trip.

Called Miss Mary so
Aaliyah walks LaKecia home.

Stayed late after school, ate dinner with
residential girls.
Ashley showed me the dorms.
It felt a little sad.

Fifteen girls without parents or grands.
Mrs. Miller supervises them.
Sort of lonely, I think.

Today After School

we walk to the art museum.
Ashley, Isabelle, Kelsey,
and me.

We rollin' Bidwell squad
four girls deep.
What I always wanted to do.

We talk all the way.
We laugh all the way.
Music, art, books, stories.
Another great day.
The bougie life for me!

I Tell LaKecia

Sometimes Grandma
gets on my nerves!
Always acting like a saint.
Wanting us
to be something better
than what she ain't.
Why can't we have internet
like normal people!

> *Why you acting thick in the head?*
> LeKecia asks.

What's wrong with you, LaKecia?
You heard what I said.

LaKecia Tells Me

Few weeks at this school,
you acting all stupid.
Like you sooo much better.
Late picking me up.
Stomping Grandma's feelings.
"A" just a letter!
I do good in school too!

I say,
She never reads
what I write!
No matter the grade.
Always say, not tonight.
Asking to be read to.

You always making her feel bad!

I'm not, I'm just mad.

Don't You Know?

Grandma can't read.
Daddy told me so, LeKecia says.

That's not true! I say.
How come Daddy told you?

Maybe he thought you knew.
But learning takes time.
A lot of work.
She doesn't always understand.
Remember you told me,
longer you do it, the better you get?

Yeah?

What does Grandma do? Hair, cooking,
and cleaning houses.
She didn't like school.
But you do.
Stop being mean.
She loves me and you.

iPhone Friend

I like Ashley—she's cool.
She wants to hang out every day.
She asks about new
"black words."
She says,
>   *I love rap.*

We don't listen to rap at home.
Ashley's confused, looking funny faced.

I say,
>   *Grandma say rap is vulgar and devilish.*

Ashley, holding her iPhone, says to follow her.

Poor Girl Dreams

Follow her where?

Snap-Story!

I say,
I don't have Snaps.

She looks more confused.
I'm trying to think of a lie.

Don't you have a phone?

I shrink, feeling high-key poor-girl.

I say,
*My phone broke. My Grandma
won't give me another until
I get a job!*

I feel my pain in my lie.

Old Phone Dreams

Ashley says,
> *That sucks.*
> *How do you talk to friends?*
> *Or do anything?*

I tell the truth:
> *I don't really have any friends.*
I take out my phone.
> *And I got this!*

Now Ashley's like high-key disgusted.

> *Yuck, it's sooooo old.*
> *What does she expect*
> *you to do with that?*

I answer her question
the best I know how:
> *Always stay embarrassed?*

New Friend

Ashley asks me about boyfriends.
I've only kissed Miles Johnson
after church youth service.

Ashley asks,
>   *You're a virgin?*

She's not.

Says,
>   *That's cute. You're like a good girl?*

I answer,
Yeah, I go to church.

Ashley says,
>   *Wow, okay.*

I think I have a new friend.

T(hat) H(o) O(ver) T(here) Goals

Ashley wanna be a *video-girl*
for Halloween.
Dancing in stripper shoes,
wearing a midriff mini.
Says she'll get lots of likes,
especially if she posts right.

Girls round my way
wanna be *video-girls*
every day!
Reality TV, music videos—
their THOT manual.

See girls tryna dance,
see girls shake and twerk,
see girls tryna be thottest.

Tryna be seen.
Tryna get attention.
Tryna be hottest.
Tryna get money.

Family Goals

Grandma says,
> *Somebody spending cash*
> *might wanna own you.*
> *Better take care yourself.*
> *Educate and own yourself!*

> *Your grandpa*
> *was a big-spender,*
> *talented dreamer.*

> *I dropped out,*
> *got pregnant.*
> *Sixteen having your daddy.*

> *My mama, fifteen,*
> *having me.*

> *Your daddy, seventeen,*
> *having you.*

Grandma says
I gotta break a curse.

Ashley Has Credit Cards

More than one.
I get whatever I save
from Saturday's hair
and Aaliyah's fake tutoring.

Ashley buys whatever she wants
at Pizza Palace every afternoon.
Sometimes a whole pizza pie!
Gossiping on haters.
Bragging about Europe.
Remembering Spain,
getting with *some* boy.
Ashley helps me with homework,
doing math problems in her head.

Pizza Palace Has Wi-Fi

for my homework.
I have to get LaKecia
before 6:00.
Or else she'll
get me in trouble
with after-school care.
LaKecia'll call Grandma,
Grandma'll call me
on the dumb
candy-bar phone, yelling.

Ashley says she wishes she had
a real family,
a real home.

Someplace
to laugh and cry
together.

Grandma's Lessons

Ashley's different than my
friends from middle school.
Way different from Aaliyah!
Grandma says, *Folks grow
like their parents.
Apples don't fall
far from the tree.*

Grandma says
that's why I write,
why LaKecia sings
beautifully.
On account of Mama
and Daddy's talents.

I tell Grandma about
Ashley's credit cards,
Pizza Palace, and her daddy.

Then Grandma starts on her
apple stories again!

Apples and Potatoes

Grandma says,
Every apple's different though.
That's uniqueness
in the Universe.
So many different apples.
But they all apples.

Be careful, 'cause
when you peel
and cut it,
apples look like potatoes.
Some folks acting
friendly ain't friends.
You should spend more time
with your other friends,
like Aaliyah.
She be needing a friend,
like you.

Ashley Says

I knew I was loved,
ya know?
More than caring about
money or things.
Those other girls don't understand
like you...
My mom's death woke me up!

Says,

Stupid girls only think about shopping, clothes, boys.

You don't care about those things?
I ask.

She says,

Yeah, but it's easy for me to, right?
My mom told me how things work.
Separation through segregation,
keeping black people apart.
Her parents and other white families
got much bigger head-starts.

Time Dreams

Ashley says,

> *Dad gives money*
> *instead of time.*
> *Time is money.*
> *"Where's the return on this investment, Ashley?"*
> *His question*
> *when I request visits.*
> *I wish he'd died instead of my mom...*

I say I understand
(but I really don't).
I wish...

> *What?*

But instead of answering I smile,
eat pizza,
my eyes rolling crazy.

Grandma's Phone Is Smart

Not as smart as Ashley's though.

I'll buy one soon,
doing hair with Grandma
and fake tutoring Aaliyah.

Our landline
is for Daddy.

When he's in prison,
          we can't call Daddy when we want.
Have to wait until
          he has telephone privileges.
Then he calls Grandma collect,
          or with the phone-card Grandma puts money on.

Letters Are Better

When I hear Daddy's voice,
my throat tightens.
All my tears fall out.
LaKecia doesn't cry
until after good-byes.

I love reading letters over again.
Smelling them.
Holding them.

Telephone calls
just fade

away.

LaKecia Wants to Know

How come Aaliyah paying you
for doing your own homework?

Mind ya business!

When you get in trouble it izz my bizzinessss!

Next Wednesday, Aaliyah's gone before I get to the
Center.
Next Monday, no Aaliyah.
Ask around, but nobody's seen her.
Miss Mary calls the house.
Aaliyah run away.

Party Night

Friday is Big Academy Night!

We'll spend the night in school.
A party.

PARTY-PARTY-PARTY

Games, movies, karaoke!
Never did karaoke.

Grandma says I can go as long as
chores Saturday,
church Sunday.

Been at Bidwell for two months.
Everybody likes me!

#PIZZAPALACENIGHTMARE

Out of nowhere,
a ghost appears.
My mama.
Pale-skinned.
Pencil thinned.

Brown sweater,
gray mini-skirt.
Hair slicked back
like it hurt.

Face revealing
sunken cheeks.
Dark-circled eyes.
Reddened knees.

Her skin dry,
she knocks and shouts.

My mama Lisa
calls me out.

I turn my head,
look away.
I'm feeling shook.
Should I stay?

Wanna run,
wanna hide.
Feeling trapped,
I stay inside.

All a sudden,
who do I see?
Miss Thomasina,
Mama's "get high" buddy.

She leaves the window.
They jump in a car,
zoom down the parkway.
That is all.

Ashley asks,
    Who was that?

Pipe Dream Lies

I say,
Nobody. A junkie from round my way.

> Ashley says,
> *She knows you?*

Neighbors know me.

> *I thought your neighborhood was, like, black.*

Neighborhood's not a color. Besides, everyone who's black don't look black.

> *Oh yeah. Like Cardi B?*

Yeah, I say,
like Cardi B.

I'm angry. Not at Ashley.
Just angry.

Angry for all the time Mama street-ghosting,
          copping, and hustling.

Rewards of Lying

Before we go to Bidwell Academy Night,
Ashley says,
>   *I have a surprise for you!*

Climb stairs to the school rooftop.
Wine bottle waiting.
Small paper-wrapped package,
Nikki written on top.

Who's Nikki?

>   *It's you, silly!*
>   *Your nickname.*
>   *Open it!*

An iPhone!

I'm shook.
Who gives away iPhones?

Grandma won't let me keep this.
Can't afford service.
Thanks, though.

Ashley says,
It's not new,
seven years old.
Just don't tell her.

Case has your nickname!

Flip side reads
Nikki in rhinestones.

Thank you,
I say,
not feeling nicknames
but happy just the same.

Red Wine Dreams

Ashley says,
You can still Snap or Insta over wi-fi!

I'm like, so excited!

I still can't believe you gave me an iPhone.

It's not a big deal.
They're like, fifty dollars on eBay.

She says it
like $50 is 50 cents.

New-to-me iPhone!
I wrap arms around Ashley, fall over.
Laughing, she shows me
how to use this great gift.

We drink rooftop red wine.
Ashley names stars.

The Wine Is Nasty

Don't like it.
Say I like it though.
Drink because
Ashely says,
    OMG! It's delicious!

I'm singing, laughing.
Ashley's laughing.
Instagramming drunk selfies.
Drunk storytelling.
Laughing with her phone.

We miss karaoke,
spend hours on rooftop,
drunk social media making.

Would She?

Ashley shares secrets about
Kelsey, Justine, & Isabella.
Former BFFs.
Frenemies now.

Would she share my secrets
to someone else?

Will she hate me too?
If she learns the truth?

Am I making it bad for
the next girl who looks
like me?

Do I have responsibility
just because I'm the only
black girl she's friends with?

Ashley Never

calls me by my real name.
The name my father says is special…

She says,

> Come on, Nikki's easy!

Then,

> You are my only true
> friend, the only one
> I can be myself with.

Are we really friends?
Really, truthfully?
Can't tell her my truth.

Message from God

Taking part in charades is lying, actively!
Playing charades stops honesty.
Stops true friendship.
Admit lying.

Pastor's Sunday message.
God must have told him I'm lying.
But I understand how Ashley feels, sort of.
Sometimes I wish Mama was dead.

Will God forgive me?

Nobody's business what my truth is
when I leave these streets.

LaKecia Finds My iPhone

> *Who's Nikki, and why you got her phone?*

Stop taking my stuff!

LaKecia bed bouncing,
one hand toward the ceiling.
The other pushes me!

> *I'ma scream, tell!*

I'm Nikki! It's my phone!

I grab her legs.

> *You ain't!*
> *Whose iPhone this is?*

A nickname,
a gift. Give it back!

> *From your rich bff?*

Give it back!

> *Daddy said, don't let nobody*
> *call you out your name.*

Well, he ain't here, is he?

Change of Plans

Grandma, you said I could trick or treat with Ashley!

> *My plans changed. I got*
> *Sisters Fellowship.*

But I made plans!

> *You're Oni.*

You're Grandma.

> *Excuse me?*

I'm tired of doing your job!
I hate you!

Punishment

First time
Grandma slapped me,
phone got disconnected
talking to Daddy.

Started screaming, couldn't stop.

Second time,
last year, eighth grade graduation,
Mama absent.
Later, Mama shows up
high.
Grandma calls cops,
Mama leaves.

I shoulda stopped screaming,
so I got slapped.

Third time's alarming.

Broken Dreams

Have to stay with LaKecia.

No longer about this
Community Center
life.

Grandma praying with
Jesus's "Sisters" in church.

LaKecia mad at me.
I'm mad at her.
Don't need to be here.
Lots of counselor-babysitters here.
LaKecia a'ight,
got friends.

Gonna slip home,
snatch Grandma's
wig, and
jet!

New to Me

Got my new-to-me iPhone,
Ashley's paid-return Uber.
Won't get caught.

Do hair & makeup
—lit!

Helping with my stoned
prep-school BFF's
Halloween THOT costume.

Wine tastes good now!

Hate Mama's lies!
Say it out loud to the sky!
Hate Grandma's rules!
Hate both of you!

Drunken Truth

We take selfies.
We tell our drunken truths.

Shanequa: *Hate everybody! Except you, Ashley.*
You take the funnest, beautiful-est pictures ever.

Ashley: *I hate my dad!*

Shanequa: *Hate my dad, too!*

Ashley: *I hate my mom!*

Shanequa: *Wish my mom were dead!*

Ashley: *She is. You're drunk!*

Shanequa: *Yeah, my mom's a junk-head.*

Nightmare Sparks

Shanequa: *Only wished she was dead.*
Little friend fib.
Forgive me?

Ashley: *Huh?*

Shanequa: *Grandma says*
Mama's a sick sinner.
Left us after Daddy committed murder.

Ashley: *What?*

Shanequa: *My mom burns her dreams.*
Flicking lighters, inhaling deep,
exhaling steam.
Life trapped in sleep.

Ashley: *What? You lied? Your mom's alive?*

Vomit Dreams

Uber text dings.
Drunken truth makes me
    feel sickly.

The roof's spinning.
Ashley just stares toward stars.
She weaves, gulping the last wine drops.
She heaves,
    vomiting over the roof ledge.
Grandma's prettiest wig flies off her head,
    meeting the vomit-stained sidewalk.

Ashley says,
GO AWAY!

10:00pm

LaKecia waits outside
Grider Community Center
alone.

Cigarette spirits fly.
Smoky shadows
searching for something
to smash street sickness.
Seconds pass.

Lisa sees her youngest
walking alone in darkness.
Hugs heal hurt hearts.
Hand-holding keeps them warm.
Lisa remembers a happy past
while walking LaKecia home.

I Sleep

in the Uber.
Driver shakes me.
On my feet, walking home,
    upstairs.
Head spins, wishing
for bed.

LaKecia!
LAKECIA!?

Forgotten duty.
Grandma yells
sirens.
Drunken eyes roll.
Grandma's hand raises quick.
Mama says,

    Don't!

    Protects her
    winey daughter.

Grandma Asks

How could I forget LaKecia?
Who do I think I am?
What happened to her wig?
When did I become a thief?

Mama tries to help me.

Grandma yells,
> *Lisa, get out my house!!*

LaKecia is crying.
Begging Grandma to let Mama stay.
Mama starts to leave.
I whisper,
Good riddance.
LaKecia hears me.
> *It's all your fault!*
she says.

She's right. I don't care.
(I'm high-key lying.)

I Want Mama to Stay

Low-key miss Mama.
For the first time
in a long time,
I can really see Mama's face.

The sadness,
mixed with lots of pain.

Sort of what I see
in Ashley's face
when I look at our
drunk selfies.

My Own Mama

Elizabeth "Lisa" Clarke Stephens.
Former hood beauty.
Current ratchet queen.
She's scanning the apartment,
her dark eyes
swollen from tears.
Red from no sleep,
crusty with
week-old makeup.

Second-skin jeans
sized too small
to fit LaKecia.
Revealing her drug life.
Walking zombie.

The Truth?

I am repulsed.
    I hate her
    and
    I love her.
    I want her home
    here,
    with us.

After Mama leaves,
Grandma commands us
to wash up, go to bed.
Grandma walks outside.

Hear her calling to Mama.
LaKecia and I sneak,
opening the door.

Sliver-Sliced Door

open to listen in.

Grandma tells Mama about
putting drugs before us
after Daddy's conviction.

Mama must have this
yakety-yak memorized.
Do adults change hearing this?
Kids don't.

I tell LaKecia,
> *Go to the bathroom already!*
> *Wash up.*

Slowly, LaKecia walks away.

She doesn't need to hear Grandma
fuss at Mama again.
Then Grandma does a
weird 180 turn.

Grandma Tells Mama

We're having a surprise birthday party
    on Saturday for LaKecia.

Tells her,
        Clean yourself up and get over here,
        on time, sober.
        Don't embarrass these babies
        in front of their friends, you hear?

Mama tries to give Grandma a hug.
But Grandma pushes her away.

Don't You Wanna

Mama smells stale.

>Grandma says,
>*You got somewhere to take a bath, Lisa?*

Mama says,
On the list at the shelter.

>*For tonight?*

Be alright. You know me.

>*That's the problem, Lisa, I know you.*
>*Don't you wanna change, girl?*
>*Don't you wanna be their mama again?*

See Mama deflating,
crying.
Like a baby.

Couch Dreams

Grandma lets Mama inside.

Says,

> *Take yourself a shower after the girls in bed.*
> *Don't want no foolishness, now.*
> *You done broke every heart in this*
> *here house. Don't make me a fool,*
> *giving you another chance.*

Grandma turns to the door.
I slide so fast,
crash into bed.

Magic Trick

Not believing what I saw.
LaKecia keeps asking questions.

Be quiet! Before Grandma hears.
Gives us both a pre-birthday bash.

Don't wanna tell her
what I think is happening.
In case it's all part of my
drunken nightmare.

A fantastic fantasy
freeing feelings
from false
faith.

I Don't Look

at Ashley in school.
Ashley don't look at me.
Nobody talks to me
all day.
Kelsey, Isabelle, and Justine
sit with Ashley at lunch.
Catching glances at me.
When I look up,
they snicker and turn away.
Ashley told them about my lies.
Clearheaded truths about
Mama and Daddy.

Threatening Dreams

about my Mama and Daddy.
I can tell
why everyone is staring,
whispering, all day.
I remember how she
slut-shamed Kelsey.
Gossiped on Isabelle
selling Molly and
Adderall.
Threatened to put them
on Facebook blast.

Now she's friendly
with them again
just to get me mad.

Liar, Liar

Headmistress Whitaker's office.
Ashley inside.

Told Mrs. Whitaker
I refuse to return her iPhone.

>Mrs. Whitaker asks,
>*Is this true, Shanequa?*

No.

>*You don't have it?*

I mean, yes, I have it, but—

>Ashley says,
>*She's a liar too!*

>Mrs. Whitaker says,
>*Ashley, please.*

I say,
Ashley didn't ask for it.

>*Is that true, Ashley?*

>Ashley says,
>*She's lying.*

Whitaker looks close at me.
Like Grandma.

Whitaker says,
Shanequa, the phone.

I place the new-to-me
iPhone on Whitaker's desk.

Whitaker quotes honor code:
Respect Bidwell Academy,
respect Bidwell sisters,
respect yourself.

Feeling like awaking
from dreams.
Leaving the office,
girls outside the door.
Looking. Trying not to look.
Thank goodness
it's Friday.

Twilight Zone

Home's another world.
A twilight zone.
Mama cleaned up,
smelling like a mom.
Grandma got her washing dishes.
She's singing, loud.

Grandma's the same, though.
She's on guard,
preparing for Mama
to drop another shoe.
LaKecia happy,
like Miss Mary winning the lotto.

Clock seconds
ticking out time.
This some make-believe?
Wish I had some wine…

Bus Stop

Can't be happy.
Instead, just play cool?
Don't know how to feel
no more.

Like Grandma.
Waiting, thinking, knowing
Mama gonna disappoint us
again.

Just don't know when
or how this time.
But it always comes.

Like the bus.
Might be late,
but sooner or later
it'll get there.

Our Apartment's Filled

for LaKecia's
birthday party.
She's pretending surprise.
Hard surprising someone
who sees and hears
everything.

Got good gifts.
Tablet?
We getting wi-fi?
Karaoke speaker and mic.
Clothes, bag, jewelry,
body spray, bubbles.

Miss Mary
give LaKecia a PS4
and two games!
Everybody give gift cards.
LaKecia got bank!

Karaoke Party

Karaoke started the party!
Moving the room!
Folks are taking turns singing.
Everybody's dancing.

At Miss Mary's request,
Mama sings
Mary J. Blige.

She's shaky at first,
but she warms into a fire.

So beautiful.
Looks like singing fills her up.
Folks chant,
clap for more.

Mama's joy-coated smile.

Before Miss Mary Leaves

she tells Grandma
Aaliyah's picked up.

> *Locked her up in youth detention.*
> *You pray for me, Cora. I don't know what to do.*

Act like I don't hear.

Grandma saw my neck turn.

> *You know Aaliyah's in a gang?*

No, ma'am.

> *Don't you lie to me.*

Didn't know.

Knew something.
Getting better at this game.
Grandma looking all through
and all around me.

History Dreams

Folks leave.
Daddy calls.
Got the bedroom phone
with LaKecia.
Grandma got the kitchen phone
with Mama.
Can't lie,
I'm high-key excited.
Like before everything got bad.
Like Daddy's touring with the band again.
Mama's staying home.

We get old-school family love.

Rehab Promise

Daddy asking for
alone talk
with Mama
before he gets cut off.

Lie, punk-shush LaKecia.
Put the phone on mute.

Daddy puts pressure on Mama.
Talking drug rehab.
Planting trust seeds,
watering faith.
She's making
teary promises.
They're crying.
Saying I'm sorry's.
Still in love.

Mama's quiet all night.

LaKecia's Prayers

Thanks for the party,
Daddy's phone call,
and Grandma being merciful
to Mama.

She makes Mama kneel beside her.
Found Mama a twin-zee dress
for church
in the morning.

Mama ties LaKecia's
headscarf for her.
Won't let her do mine.
Grandma taught me to care for my hair,
four years now.

I'm independent.

Don't Know

how to feel.
Wish I could act
like LaKecia, like
everything is okay.
Like tomorrow gonna be better.

But, don't know
if it's true.

If Mama's for real
this time, or
she waiting for a opening
to bounce.

LaKecia Dreams

LaKecia says,
How come you stay mad at Mommy?

Don't want to destroy LaKecia's dreams.

When I'm mad,
it makes me feel bad.

I say,
Go to sleep.

When I remember being mad,
I get mad all over again.

I'm going to sleep.

Forget about it.
You're happy again.
I figure,
don't be mad at Mommy.
Forget about it,
be happy with her.

Okay.

You told me Mommy was coming back.

So?

Dreams came true. She's back!

3:00am

Gotta pee.
Mama's supposed to be
asleep on the couch.
Scared, I think
she's already gone.

Promise broken for church
and twin-zee dresses.
Stalling,
preparing for the let-down.

Can't hold
longer,
march down the hallway.
See Mama cradled on the couch.

Like she promised.

Church Dreams

Pastor is moved seeing Mama
in church today.

Asked her to sing before his sermon.
She sings
        "How I Love Calling His Name."

The people in church love that one.
Deacon Everett asked Mama
to sing a funeral next week.

LaKecia give me the
        "I told you so" look.

Hope she's right.

Adulting

Grandma wants ginger ale.
Mama and me
walk to the store.
Asking questions
we should already
know answers to.

Wanna hug her, but
keep fighting her.

She talks about Pizza Palace.
She doesn't blame me.
She's ashamed of herself.

> *Longer I don't see you,*
> *the easier to stay away.*

Adulting harder than she thought.

Smoke and Mirrors

Mama's friend, Thomasina,
is outside the store selling puppies.
I play with the pups.
She and Mama smoke cigarettes,
talk.
Thomasina's asking Mama to
go with her
somewhere.
Mama looks at me,
tells Thomasina,
        Nah.
Then she says
something else I
can't hear.

I tell Mama,
We should get back.

Thomasina says,
        What's up, lady?

And I say,
Grandma's waiting for us!

Puppy Dreams

Mama says,
LaKecia loves puppies, Shanequa!

I say,
Oh wow, no doubt!
You can afford to buy that?

Mama says,
Thomasina ain't gonna charge me!
Are you, Thomasina?

Thomasina say,
Hey, you and me, we go way back.
We settle up later?
Right?

Laughing,
we take a puppy home.

Surprise Guest

Grandma says,
I wanted ginger ale,
not a dog!

        Mama says,
        For the birthday girl!

Don't care who it's for.
No dog living here!

        Already paid.
        Cash sale. No returns!

That's your problem.

        I say,
        Grandma, please?
        Look at her eyes.

Grandma says,
Girl, dogs add fees to rent.

        I say,
        I'll pay it!

        Mama says,
        Kids need a pet, Mom.

Not Allowed

Grandma says,
No doubt kids need pets.
More importantly,
kids need their mother.
Don't get me started,
Elizabeth Clarke Stephens.
You are a guest in my house.
Bringing animals here...
dogs not allowed!
And you on probation!

    I say,
    You're scaring Sheena, Grandma.

Who Sheena?

    Our puppy!

Then we watch Sheena pee
on the living room floor.

Three Hours

Mama's acting itchy.
Like she just can't sit still.
She and Grandma argue steady,
two warriors testing wills.
See Grandma trying,
wants Mama back.
But Mama looks…
regretful,
street whispers calling.
Maybe love's holding
her back.

Mama pacing, tryna
think something to say.
Goes to bathroom.
Sheena gets out the way.

Mama leaves bathroom,
says,
      Goin' out, smoke a cigarette.

Three hours later,
Mama ain't back yet.

Somewhere Out There

LaKecia's organizing
a search party.
Grandma, me, and Sheena
ain't going nowhere.

Mama's in the nether zone.
Found Thomasina out there.

Grandma checks her money stash.
Still safely locked away.

I say,
LaKecia's birthday money?

LaKecia yells she doesn't care.
Mama can have it all!

I check LaKecia's hiding spots.
Tablet gone, cash all gone,
gift cards still here.

Another Monday Morning

LaKecia, acting sick,
can't go to school.
Grandma ain't havin' it.
Got a job to do.

Can't change Mama.
Your mama chose.

Grandma knows,
Drugs be calling,
family be losing.

She tells us,
Keep praying.
Keep trying.
Get to school!
Stop crying.

Justine and Isabelle

speak to me first period.
Kelsey asks for help
in the library.
Ashley's crew sits at
my table for lunch.
Ashley offers her iPhone.
I decline.

She hands out
fancy water bottles.
Sorta like hers.
Filled with wine.
She winks.
Cheers!

    What-tha!

She whispers,
Calm down.
It's just wine.

Sip and Swallow

We sip and swallow
until alcohol does
what alcohol does.

Sip and swallow.
Riding its chariot.
Traveling netherworlds
where everything is possible.
      And nothing is real.

Like dreams, nightmares.
Sip and swallow.
Until you know
why Mama craves…

Does she feel
like this?

Sip
swallow
dream.

Wildfires

Everything happened so fast.
Like the wildfires in California
Mrs. Earl talked about
in social studies.

Don't remember hitting Ashley.
Don't remember
her falling on the ground.
Don't remember.
I remember red, like rage.

Red, like fire.
Red, like warnings.
Red, like stop signs.
Red, like blood.

Blood

spurting out
between Ashley's fingers.
Holding her face
like it's about to fall
beside her.

She screams.
Screaming
at *me*.

She appears to be
a victim of my
violent irrational
outburst.
She points
at me.

Red Fingernails

Manicured tight.
Screaming at me
in tones never heard out her throat.

I'm bleeding! I'm bleeding!

She screams louder.
Like she never seen her own blood before.
Like bleeding's some brand-new surprise.
A squad of teachers run to help
my victim's injuries.

You broke my nose!
Ashley cries
between teary, angry eyes.
Sounds like her tongue's
expanding in her mouth.

Like...

the words
hurt in her throat.

To Mrs. Earl,
    She broke my nose!
To me,
    You are done!

Teachers and girls talking.
Blonde hair, red hair, brown hair,
straight hair, curly hair,
short, long.
Watching, listening to half a story.

Time Slows Down

Mrs. Miller talks to me.
Her lips move, but
I can't hear her.
I'm smiling.
It's so funny!
I'm laughing.
Ashley's screaming louder.
Miller's face, really funny!
I can't control myself.
>*Why are you laughing?*
>*Have you been drinking?*
Miller whispers,
>*Shanequa? Shanequa?*
>*Are you drunk?*

She Is Drunk!

Ashley says.
Smell her breath.
Check her water bottle!

Miller takes the water bottle.
I try to run, but
Miller's got hold.
Now it clicks.
Ashley's plans
didn't include her bloodied face.
Just wanted me expelled.

She's screaming–
    Call my dad! CALL MY FATHER!

I know I'm outta here,
for good.

Flashback

Dad saying,
> *Killing that man was self-defense.*
The courts didn't believe him.
> *I'm a victim of our world,*
he said.

Blood drips
on Ashley's sweater.
Evidence of my crime.

Was my water bottle
the only one filled with wine?

Whitaker Calls Grandma

Tells her I've been drinking.
I am in school drunk.
Tells her underage drinking must be reported.
Hands me the telephone.

Take the phone, Shanequa.

I don't.

Mrs. Stephens, we'll be
contacting the police
if you don't appear.
We have zero tolerance at
Bidwell Girls Academy!

Whitaker Demands

Talk to your grandmother!

I take the telephone.

Grandma?

        She telling the truth? You been drinking?

I don't know.

        What you mean? Either yes or no.

Yes,
I cry.

        Don't know what you're thinking.
        I ain't leaving work early to come get you.

Yes Ma'am

Yes ma'am. I know.

> *You think getting drunk at school*
> *supposed to fix your mama?*

No, ma'am.

> *Girl, why you go and do*
> *something so foolish?*
> *Didn't I tell you to act right?*
> *Didn't I? Huh?*

Yes, ma'am.

> *Ain't I tell you*
> *everybody friendly ain't friends?*

Yes, ma'am.

I'm Sorry, Grandma

No use crying over spilt milk now.
You made your bed.
Gonna have to lie in it.
I guess you grown now.

I'm not, Grandma.

Huh?

I'm not grown, Grandma.

Got that right. Thought you's smarter.
How I'm gonna take care LaKecia and work?
Out here acting like your mama
and your daddy?

I'm sorry, Grandma.

Me too, Shanequa. Me too.
What's done sure enough done.

I cry.

Shanequa Oni Stephens in God's hands.
This gonna be your biggest test.
Learn for yourself to be yourself.

I'm sorry, Grandma.

Me, too.

Police

Police come.
Police come through.
Police come through the door.
Police come through the door for me.

Handcuffs on wrists.
Mrs. Miller uses a sweater
to disguise the handcuffs.

Everyone knows
what they are
and where I'm going.

Rumors Are Spreading

Whispers through the hallways.
    Shanequa is in handcuffs.
    Shanequa is going to jail.
    Shanequa is a ghetto girl.
    Shanequa is a hood rat.
    Shanequa is ratchet.
    Shanequa is a criminal.

    Ashley told us,
    we already knew it.

Ashley betrayed Justine.
She betrayed Kelsey.
She betrayed Isabelle.
Tit for tat?

I Was Always Told

consequences are simple
for those
who call you outta name.
No matter who believes,
show haters where you stand.

Some folks don't get it.
Some folks don't understand
why this word fills up pain.
When
we
hear it time and time
again.

Some hear it
playfully in streets.
Ain't play all games?

Ashley wasn't playing,
her eyes got
bigger,
opened her mouth
called me,
N***er!

My fists clenched tight.
Didn't hold back, cracked her nose.
Reaction attack.

I Am

I know
I am a human
being.
Proud member
of this race.
I stand strong and
tall.
I punched
her in her face.

I am not an ugly curse.
I am my father's dream.
I stand here,
expect the worst.
I wish it was a dream.

Youth Detention Center

I enter through metal detectors,
emptying pockets,
recite and spell my name.
Two giant steel doors.
One in front.
One behind.
Wait in this small locked space.
Separated from the entrance.
Wait until the
second giant steel door before us opens.
An entrance to a new world.
Slamming thunderstorms
behind me.

I Jump

feeling the echo in my feet
as the doors shut.
Sound reminder.
> The end of everything good.
Beginning something bad.
I am scared.
High-key-horror-movie-end-
of-the-real-world-devil-hell-fire scared.
Is Grandma coming?
Just want to see her,
even if she yells.

Once in County Youth Detention

your own clothes are taken away.
You're given a poly/cotton jumpsuit.
Navy blue.
How many girls wore this one?
Soap, deodorant,
one pair white cotton socks,
every other day.
Fresh white cotton underwear,
every day.

Blanket, sheet,
pillow, pillowcase.
Brown rubber flip-flops.
Toothbrush, comb, or pick
given in morning and evening.

Youth detainee must
return toothbrush, comb, or pick to the
Youth Detention Worker
(a.k.a. YDW)
after each use.

Chump-Punk Dreams

Cells are as
big as my bathroom at home.
YDWs control lights
and locks.
Need permission
to use the bathroom.
6am wakeup.
10:30pm bedtime.
Sitting on a bed
bolted to the wall.
Thin plastic-covered mattress,
half-glass door.

Such a chump,
such a punk,
getting brought down
like this.
        Don't cry.
Don't show weakness.

The YDWs

tell me,
> *Take out your braids.*

Give me a paper bag
to put my hair inside.
Hair Grandma added
with mine.

I'm wishing for Grandma's kitchen.
Hard chair, lavender Pine-Sol,
turnip greens, cornbread.

Love.

Feeling Grandma's care,
remember fingertips touch,
pulling my scalp
whichever direction needed
to finish the job.

Family Disconnect

Picking out hair braids,
taking out perfect patterns
carefully crafted
by Grandma's hands.

Each moment's unbraiding
hurts my heart.
Daydreaming about yesterdays,
while disconnecting braids
from the braider's work.

Something smells familiar—
shame.

Girls' Pod

Miss Denise and Miss Barbara are
the YDWs managing the
girls' pod.

Pods contain cells and common area.
On the right, a desk for YDWs.
Telephone, notepads, pencils,
electric sharpener, floor safe.

Four closed
toilet rooms on the left
with sinks, soap, and
electric dryers.

New Girl

Four enclosed
shower rooms on the right.
None of the rooms in the pods
lock from the inside.

Miss Denise tells me,

Attention everyone!
This is Shanequa.
Introduce yourselves.
Her first time.
Remember your first time and be kind.

Pod Mates

Two girls
on a sofa in the far left corner
look up from a PlayStation game.
  Whatever.

Two girls
playing UNO at one of
the four tables bolted to the floor.
One looks up.
  S'up.

The other, her back turned,
steady looking at her cards
like she deaf to sound.

Another Girl

reading at another table
raises her eyes, getting glimpses.

Another
pacing in a cell.

All a sudden, some girl yells,

>   *UNO! HA! I win, I win!*

She turns.
>   *Shanequa?*
>   *That you?*
>   *SHANEQUA STEPHENS?*

Before I Can Answer

toilet flushes.
Little freckle-faced, round,
peach-colored girl
walks toward me.

Call me Pinto!

Miss Denise says,
No, your name's Mariah.

Miss Denise, Pinto ain't no gang name.
My grandad nicknamed me.
I done told you!

And I told you.
Your birth name
is your name here.
Remember?

Talking Fast

like a bumblebee
avoiding rain,
is a girl named Mariah.

What's your name?
Couldn't hear in the bathroom...

Her name's Shanequa,

says Aaliyah. She stands here,
two inches taller since last
we talked.

Mariah Says

I gotta cousin name Shanequa,
half-cousin.

> Aaliyah says,
> *Leave her alone, Mariah.*

Huh?

> *You all up in her face! Let her breathe fresh air.*

My breath stinks?

> *Yes!*

My breath don't stink!

Everybody laughs.
Aaliyah in charge here.

> *Yo, y'all, Shanequa my homie.*
> *Her daddy hood famous!*
> *We fam, you feel me?*

She gives me a wink.

> *Don't be 'fraid, a'ight?*
> *Nobody gonna mess with you.*

Aaliyah Is Almost

six feet tall.
If she wanted, she could model,
but that's not her thing,
'less she's modeling with basketballs,
    which could happen.

Her daddy
Hill Street Crew.

Miss Mary and Grandma
talk on him,
call him George.

    Daddy call him
    Boogie-G.
    He was taller than Aaliyah.
    LeBron James big,
    James Harden beard.

I Remember

some summer days,
Aaliyah's dad would
buy the ice cream
truck man out.
Treat everybody in the hood.

He threw the illest
block parties
every
Memorial and Labor Day.

Bounce castles, DJ, hot dogs,
soda, Huggy-drinks, and burgers!
All night long!
Until somebody called the cops!

Miss Esther

my social worker—
she Jamaican/Haitian?—
is trying small talk.

> *Do you like Bidwell Academy?*
> *Your grades are pretty high.*

When I go home?

> *Hearing is tomorrow, 9am.*

Grandma be there?

Miss Esther got my school records.
She know my family history.

> *How long you've been drinking?*
> *You do drugs?*

Court Date

I'm wearing my own clothing
and handcuffs to court.

Court's a big, carpeted room with
long table and chairs.
Grandma waiting.
Pastor Gorham,
Mr. Lawyer, too.

Handcuffs off,
hugging Grandma.
I apologize in person.

Judge Conklin
listens to the lawyer.
Miss Esther talks
good grades,
private school,
privileged girls,
broken family.

Shanequa Ain't a Bad Girl

Grandma says.
Pastor Gorham talks
choir, youth group.

Judge talks
underage drinking,
breath and pee tests
positive for alcohol.

Assault and underage drinking
have consequences.
Recommending secure youth detention,
thirty days.

Mr. Lawyer requests mercy,
first offense.
Talks personal,
emotional, family
trauma.

Mr. Lawyer Asks

for community service.
Tells judge,
Teenage misunderstanding...

Judge reveals pictures—
Ashley's broken nose.
No deals.

Lawyer asks,
Electric ankle monitor?

Lock me up at home.
Judge says no.
Miss Esther says
Ashley used the N-word.
Grandma gasp.

Judge says,
More self-control needed.
Quotes sticks and stones.

Says, *Anger therapy requested.*
Return in two weeks.

So I stay in Detention.

Mr. Lawyer Says

That went well.

Grandma says,
How staying in jail for two weeks well?

And to me,

Why you ain't tell me Ashley call you out your name?

My face gets hot.
Eyes wanna cry.
Feel them well up.

Grandma, Esther, Lawyer
raising voices.
Pastor Gorham takes hands
for prayer.
Police walk in,
collect me.

Regular School Day in Detention

Miss Barbara brings me to
classes.

Pink-faced and skinny
lady teacher,
Miss Leonard, starts us off
science and math.

Most these girls way behind.
Some don't know
they don't know.

Hard believing in yourself
if you don't know
what you can do.

Hello Again

After five-minute bathroom break,
see the English teacher—Miss Precious!
Excited, then embarrassed.
Like, what I'm doing here?
She's cool. She don't flinch, don't stutter.

> *Good morning, ladies.*
> *Sorry I see so many*
> *familiar faces.*
> *We'll start class*
> *free-writing in journals.*
>
> *Shanequa, hello again.*

She remembers me?

> *Please pass out these journals.*

What You Mean Free Write?

Aaliyah yells out,
like on the playground.

Miss Precious says,
Write words in your mind.
Making sense is not necessary.
Write till I say stop.

I Don't Get It

Aaliyah says, pushes on her journal.
Can't think'a nothin'.

Miss Precious walks closer.
Looks Aaliyah in the eye.
Pushes her journal toward her.

What do you love?

Basketball.

*Write five lines
describing a basketball memory.*

Aaliyah writes,
*I dream about basketball all day, every day.
Pop loved b-ball. We watch TV, LeBron, or KD.
I'm his only child, so he coached me.
Gave me knowledge. I was thirsty.
Running builds endurance, shooting builds skills.*

Christine Is

the cell pacer.
Like zoo tigers.
Trying to un-puzzle
their capture.

Miss Leonard
couldn't get Christine to work.
Don't think Miss Precious
will either.

Christine don't talk.
Except for yelling
in her cell.
Last night,
heard Christine crying.

She's who you
stay away from.
A nothing-to-lose
girl.

Her journal stay closed.

Shanequa Is

numb,
feels no thing,
is away,
is gone,
is invisible.

Shanequa
is on view.
Looking at who?

Shanequa
is gone,
is not here,
is invisible,
is spirit,
is air,
no longer exists.

Shanequa is smoke.
Shanequa is fog.
Shanequa is wind.
No one understands
who or why
I am.

Poetry Assignment

Miss Precious says,

Some of you will be out tomorrow.
Some of you will be out next week.
Some of you will be out next month.
For some of you, that's good.

This poetry prompt,
"Where I'm From,"
helps you define who, what,
and where you want to be.
We'll write,
then we'll share.

Where I'm From
by Shanequa O. Stephens

I'm from the East Side,
      where cigarette wrappers
      and crushed beer cans
      roll down the street.

I'm from Michael
      and Lisa
      and Grandma Cora.

I'm from music
      and shouting in church.
      Where a choir of sleepy
      kids would rather
      be in front of a PlayStation.

I'm from
      food stamps, smoked greens,
      smothered chicken, rice, and gravy.
      Where we shop the dollar store
      the first of the month.

I'm from
      Don't cry
      over spilt milk.
      Where we make lemons
      into lemonade.

I'm from
  guilty with cause.
  Where we waste wishes
  waiting on reversing time
  where Daddy didn't shoot that gun.

I'm from
  When is mama coming home,
  and where is she?

I'm from
  Oni means big sister.
  Where I make sure LaKecia
  does homework
  and says prayers.

I'm from
  crying myself to sleep,
  trying to understand.

I'm from
  embarrassment, shame.
  Where water mixes with baby formula,
  where crack is cocaine.

I'm from
  where everyone wants to leave.
  Where we have to stay.

I'm from
  scratch, scrape, scream.
  Where you study getting ahead.

I'm from
      where anger is afraid of truth.
      Where dreams aren't remembered.
      Where secrets aren't spoken.

I'm from
      Toughen up, don't cry.
      Where you pray and sing out loud.

Gym Free Play

Aaliyah call basketball!
We count fouls, squad up.
Me, Mariah, Aaliyah
versus
Jada, Lisette, Diamante.
Christine's odd out, so
Miss Denise squad with Jada.
We got Christine.

Miss Barbara Referee

Winner's first to 12.
Jada and Miss Denise got game.
We down 2 points.

Aaliyah strategy:
After layup, tells Christine to
foul Jada. Saying,
She can't shoot a free.

Miss Barbara calls Christine's foul.
Jada throws a brick.

Aaliyah pass to me,
I pass to

Christine.

SWISH!

Jada Need the Nurse

Her wrist swelling.
Aaliyah tryna punk her,
     Christine get you like that?
Jada's face show offense.
     Ooh, she mad!
     Look, she mad!
Miss Denise on alert.
     Alright everybody, let's line up.
     Aaliyah, enough.

Christine Fouled Jada Hard

I saw.
Now, Christine smiling.
Jada see,
she ain't having it. Says,
   Tryna play me?

Miss Barbara and Miss Denise
cross between all of us,
a reminder of where we are.
   Alright ladies, squashing this.
   Line up.

Miss Barbara takes Jada to nurse.
Us line up,
hands behind our backs.

Group with Miss Esther

Miss Esther asks,
Why do you think you're here?

Diamante says her
mom and boyfriend
smoke crack in their house.

Cops find a weed plant
inside Diamante's room.

　　　Me and sisters go foster care.

Cuts class, algebra.

　　　Don't do math good.

She and her BFF hang
in park until
science class, next period.

　　　Had gold sharpie,
　　　You know, like I'm drawing
　　　on the bench.

Police pick her up.
Graffiti and truancy charges.

　　　Plus, I had some weed on me.

My Turn

Shanequa Oni, my given name.

Not what Ashley hissed
before her face
slammed my fist.

Flipping emotional switch.
Shading hate.
Cracking whips.

Growing whispers
inside my head.
Filled with anger.
Filled with dread.

Fighting words starting battles.
Fighting words creating pain.
Fighting words making scars.
Making you less a human being.

Samantha's Turn

We CHINS. Child in Need of Supervision.

Samantha been inside before.

> *Mother always trying to control me.*
> *Forever fighting and calling police.*

Samantha high on meth,
waving butcher knife.

> *What Mom expects?*
> *My mind wasn't right.*

She was gonna stab her.

> *Jealous about my "boyfriends."*
> *She always broke.*

Samantha street-money-making.
> *Mom takes my cash.*
Name-calling, slut-shaming.
> *Out like trash.*

Fight again, run away.
Walking streets,
no place to stay.
Sleep, cold, and hunger
take her places
I never want to go.

Christine's Turn

Two months ago,
Christine was 12.
Her birthday was last week,
here in the pod.
The cake was good, she said.

Saw my mom killed.
Got foster mom. She was okay.
Was old, got sick.

Another foster home,
they weren't okay.
Christine ran away.
Fought, took cash,
credit cards.
They called police.
Now detention home
today.

Lisette's Turn

Lisette's mom an RN.
She fix people.
Stepdad's a mechanic.
He fix cars.
> *My dad's invisible.*
> *He breaks my heart.*

When Lisette get mad,
she break stuff up.
Lisette's mad a lot,
never has enough.
> *Had a fight,*
> *got suspended.*

Mom took her stuff.
Thought she could end it.
A screwdriver, a hammer,
a drill on the door.
> *Broke down the closet,*
> *didn't think anymore.*

Lisette's mom got home
said, *ENOUGH!*
Volume got loud,
fighting got tough.
Couldn't hold her down.
Couldn't make her stop.
"Ring-ring" cops.

Lisette in handcuffs.

Jada's Turn

Jada mama don't allow
no disrespect.

> *Nah, nobody, yo.*
> *Ma find somebody*
> *play or whup me,*
> *SHE gonna whup my behind again.*
> *Know what I'm sayin'?*

Jada got another hard knock life.
Talking hands, patting chest.

> *That's foundation.*
> *Like bargain basement ish, there.*
> *Like what holds up buildin's.*
> *Like yo' feet, yo.*
> *Keep them joints sturdy yo.*
> *Know what I'm sayin'?*

Jada, not like these other girls out here.
Jada
           "un-play-wit-able."

Back in the Pod

Need time to think.
Need time to write.
These girls got troubles
in their life.
Thought mine was whack.
Thought I was poor.
Grateful for Grandma,
all she provided for.

Aaliyah, Me, Mariah

Goofing.

Aaliyah spits a rhyme.

> *Always trying to foul me out.*
> *Always brickin', your shot is blocked.*
> *Always all up in my face.*

She stuck, so I freestyle.

Always walking a baller's race.

> *Oh!*

Always trying, misunderstood.
Always tomorrow in the 'hood.

> *Woah!*

Always running, this ain't home.

Mariah shut it down.

Always Mariah.
I'm a rock-hard stone.

> *Ho! That was hot!*

Visiting Hours

Pastor Gorham and LaKecia visiting.

Where's Grandma?

> Pastor says,
> *She doesn't want to see you in here.*

Want me punished?

> *You disappointed her.*
> *You disappointed all of us.*
> *She'll always love you.*
> *Family always gives us second chances.*

LaKecia gives me two letters.

Daddy's Letter

Dear Shanequa Oni,

Sorry I'm not with you.
Haven't given you the best life.
Made some bad choices.
Don't follow my path.
Tried teaching y'all.
Tried protecting my family.
My biggest crime.

DON'T follow our footsteps.
You gotta build strong boots with rubber soles.
You gotta jump high and bounce.

Love,
Daddy

Mama's Letter

Dear Baby-girl,

Apologizing.
You deserve better.
I shoulda put my children first.
You loved me no matter what.
You're perfect.
Always smiling, happy, laughing.
I'm ashamed I
took your sparks away.
Didn't know how to be
without your daddy.
Was afraid to get help.
I love you. Hope you can forgive me.

I love you,
Mama

You'll Be Home Soon

LaKecia says.
Shanequa, I feel it.
Grandma and Sheena are BFFs now.
Taught her some tricks.

I say,
Tell Grandma I miss her.
I'm gonna write a poem just for her.
Will you read it to her?

You know it!

Why you crying?

I said I'd read it.

Pastor says,
LaKecia, she loves you.

True? You crying 'cause you love me?

I'm Not Like No Other

I'm writing.
Hear hollering.

> *Know what I'm sayin'?*
> *Not soft, yo. Won't take it. Christine can't play Jada.*
> *Know what I'm sayin'? Girly, lil girl.*

See Jada tryna get up in Christine's face.

> *Huh, what? You sayin' something? Huh, what?*

Miss Barbara call for Miss Denise on the walkie-talkie.

> *Jada eat a Christine before breakfast. All day every day,*
> *yo!*

Miss Barbara tryna get between them.
Christine don't say nothin', Jada gettin' louder.

> *Christine a Jada snack. What? Disrespect me?*
> *What? Is you sick, girl? Not take your vitamins?*
> *Jada un-play-wit-able!*

Christine's got Jada in chokehold.
Jada making animal sounds.
Kicking and scratching whoever's close.

Lockdown

Girls chant.
Miss Barbara yells,
Lockdown!
Alarms go off. Lights flash.
We're locked in cells.
YDWs march in,
geared up.

Miss Esther Group Session, Pt. 2

Lisette gone home.
Diamante to placement.
Samantha gone to treatment.

Christine and Jada in isolation
until further notice.

Aaliyah say Jada started.
Mariah said Christine ended.

Miss Esther ask what I think.

I'm Emotional

Talk about
words revealing shame
for my parents.
For myself.

I'm being straight up.

I played Ashley,
then I got played.

My parents are
human beings.
Human beings make mistakes.
That's how we learn.

Like you, you know,
like me,
like everybody.

Aaliyah Disagrees

Later, Aaliyah says,
> Was me, 'stead a you?
> She call me outta name like that?
> Shoot, be a murder bid.

I say,
She was not worth that!

> *I hear you.*

Some words got real strong meanings,
especially you change tones.
Put history up in there…
Words speak to kill, right?

> *Word.*

Set Up

But Aaliyah,
check this out.
It's all a setup.

    How you mean?

I played myself
over somebody else's
words.
I'm a writer.
Spoken word.
Just breath, invisible.
Temporary.
Poof-gone.
Ashley's breathin' fresh air and
I'm here.
Instead'a kicking it
with LaKecia.
Writing songs on the keyboards.

Pride and shame.
Revolving-door,
old-school game!

My Letter

Dear Judge,

Wanted to be liked.
Wanted to belong.
Felt deprived,
seeing what others owned.

Know I'm human.
Know I'm great.
But so much history,
fear, and shame
made me fake.

Sunrise a new life.
Every day wear the mask.
Drink wine and pretend
because I'm really mad.

Believing dreams.
Believe truth's name.
Shanequa Oni Stephens,
shining through rain.

Stop wasting time.
Stop speaking lies—
        I've grown.
Gotta revolution
in mind.
        I'm ready to go home.

Miss Precious Says

You want to help your family,
friends?
Yourself?
Share feelings, thoughts, and dreams!

Dream, make, do.
Tell your truth.
How you feel—
that's truth.

You're gifted, Shanequa.
Share that greatness and
continue being great!

I have applications for
Alternative Performing Arts High,
a music and art school.

Take one!

Hearing Day

Grandma sitting
with Pastor and Mama.
Mama wearing the twin-zee church dress.
Gained weight.

Grandma did her hair.
Full, natural, springy,
rusty brown shiny coils
frame her face.
Mr. Lawyer presents proof of
Mama's treatment.
She, Grandma, LaKecia in family therapy.
Grandma taking literacy classes.
Getting her GED!

Miss Esther talks about
group therapy progress.

Court Ruling

Miss Precious's letter says:

Dear Judge Conklin,

Shanequa Oni Stephens
has shown an outstanding
ability to create.
Shanequa's poems have
meaning, strength, and power.
Writing honestly about the
painfully difficult
is her gift.

Judge gives an honor speech.

I go home today!

Really Home

Grandma gets out of her
new-to-her car.
Touching my hair.
Flipping through Instagram
hairstyles we'll try.

(After I work off her
stolen wig.)

Sheena learning to roll over
and begging.

Pastor Gorham took Mama
to the treatment facility.

She has a curfew until
she's finished.

Mama got a facility job.

It's good being home.

Dream Big

An Alt Arts student now.
    Aaliyah, yeah,
    she in my crew.
We squad-writing lyrics.
    Got some lit beats too.
Had some hard knocks.
Had some trouble,
        made mistakes.
But look at me now,
    I'm a writer rhyming great.
I'mma tell y'all the truth.
    I'mma spill all the tea.
Believe in yourself,
    cause that's who you GOTTA be.
My daddy told me, girl,
    when life beats you down,
gotta pick yourself up.
    Gotta lift off the ground.
Gotta build strong boots.
    Be the brand that you trust.
Yo, tie them laces tight.

    You can bounce straight up!

WANT TO KEEP READING?

If you liked this book, check out another book

from West 44 Books:

FIFTEEN AND CHANGE
BY MAX HOWARD

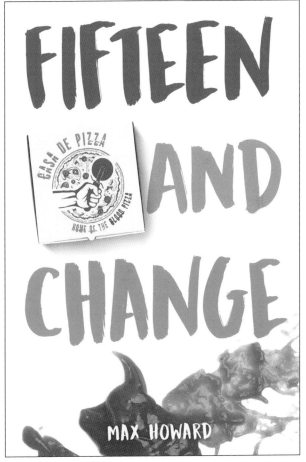

ISBN: 9781538382592

My heart pounds
like I've spotted a deer.

Breathe in,
smell pizza.
Breathe out,
phones are ringing.
Will that be for pickup or delivery?

Breathe in,
What would you like on that?
Breathe out,
try not to be
invisible.

Say:

Hey, I saw your sign outside.
You guys hiring?

ABOUT THE AUTHOR

Annette Daniels Taylor is a spoken-word artist from Staten Island living in Western New York. An Arthur A. Schomburg fellow, she studies media arts at the State University of New York at Buffalo. She is a Pink Door Poetry alum and graduate of Empire State College. The author of *Street Pharmacist* and *Hush Now... Poems to Read Aloud*, she leads spoken-word workshops with teenagers at youth detention centers modeling creative expression.

EVERY LITTLE
BAD IDEA

CAITIE MCKAY

The Same
Blood

M. AZMITIA

FIFTEEN
AND
CHANGE

MAX HOWARD

ONE
too many
LIES

L.A. BOWEN

Check out more books at:
www.west44books.com

An imprint of Enslow Publishing

WEST **44** BOOKS™